The Boy
Who Played Tiger

BY THE SAME AUTHORS

Orange-robed Boy

The Boy Who Played Tiger

Patricia Wallace Garlan and Maryjane Dunstan

Illustrated by John Pimlott

The Viking Press New York

For Robert, who knows all
about the boy who played tiger

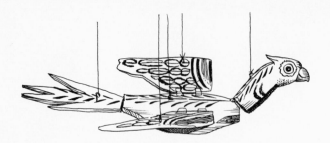

Chapter 1

Ko Shway was playing King-of-the-jungle. It was a sticky, hot day, and the fat limb of the banyan tree was slippery under the grip of his bare knees.

He sat very tall, shading his eyes from the sun as he gazed proudly out over his kingdom. His vantage point in front of his tree house in the huge banyan tree at the edge of the jungle was the highest for miles around.

"I am King Anawrahta!" he announced loudly, though there was no person in sight. "I am riding on my elephant at the head of my army."

Indicating with a proud sweep of his arm the massive jungle behind him, he shouted, "This is my army."

From his shoulder was slung a curved sword.
Wrenching it from its scabbard, he waved it above
his head and called out, "I have come to banish

my enemies and bring the Buddha to Upper
Burma!"

He glared fiercely out over the dry rice fields

stretching away before him, and pointed his sword at two water buffaloes who were wallowing, uninterested, in a leftover puddle of mud.

"You generals, there—pay heed! King Anawrahta, the greatest king in all Burma, has come to conquer you." His words rang out across the fields but evoked no response from the water buffaloes.

Ko Shway looked up and over the backs of the water buffaloes, over the rice fields, over the litttle village that was his home, to the deep jungle beyond. The jungle was before him and behind him, encircling the fields and the little village. The jungle before him was the army of the enemy, stretching away to the blue sky as far as the eye could see.

At his waist Ko Shway carried a horn made of hammered brass. It was unusually large and twisted in an odd shape. Now he raised the horn to his lips and blew with all his strength again and again, a sound big enough and strong enough to bring terror to the hearts of his enemy. He paused, listening. He could still hear the sound pulsing and echoing in the far distance. "That will show them who is king!" he said to himself.

But, as the echo faded, an answer came—a rumble, growing louder and very strong. The fearful, deep-throated sound started a pounding in Ko Shway's chest. Was that the tramp of an army marching?—the bawl of an enemy horn? Suddenly all was silent. And suddenly Ko Shway knew what he had heard: that was no roar of defiance flung by an enemy army. That was the call of a tiger.

A tiger! There had been rumors of a tiger in recent weeks. But no one had seen it. Oh, to be able to see it! It was probably deep in the jungle, though; it would not come near enough to be seen.

Ko Shway climbed off the limb and into his tree house, glad to be high up in the banyan tree. Even though the tiger was far away, it was comforting to be in a tree; tigers, unlike leopards, do not climb trees.

He flopped down on the matted floor and looked at the comfortable clutter around him. Ko Shway was a boy who liked to be doing things, and here in his tree house were reminders of old adventures. There were clackers and whistles and gongs, swords and masks and kites, and an elephant's toenail he had carved for a charm.

A huge snakeskin dangled from one of the branches which formed a ceiling. Under it, resting on a green bed of banana leaves, was the favorite of all his possessions: the head of a tiger.

Brightening, he ran his hand over the sleek head. Well, it wasn't real, but it didn't look like a paper tiger, either. He had worked on it for weeks, molding it of papier-mâché and painting it very carefully with saffron dye and charcoal dust. He had stuck in fierce whiskers which were really elephant hairs. It was hollow, so that he could put his hand right up inside the head. Its sharp teeth were carved from bone and polished white. He had faithfully copied every detail of the shape and coloring from a book about tigers belonging to U Gyi, Head Man of the village. U Gyi, whose name meant "Honorable Mr. Big," was also the only rich man in the village, and so the only person who owned books.

Ko Shway picked up some stalks of elephant grass and poked the stiff ends down through holes in the matted floor, arranging them here and there in front of the head to make it look as if it were in the jungle. He imagined for a moment that he was the tiger he had heard, slinking through the dense jungle, stalking his prey.

A tiger is lucky, he thought. He can do anything he wants to do. All the animals are afraid of him; and everywhere he goes, there is excitement. A tiger is important.

The still air pressed around Ko Shway, and the harsh mat was damp under his bare legs and feet. Ko Shway got up restlessly and climbed to the roof of his tree house. Even here it was hot.

He stripped off his shirt. His *longyi,* the long cotton skirt worn by Burmese children and adults alike, was pulled up high between his legs and tucked in at his waist. He reached with his toes and the soles of his feet to feel the coolness of the flat banyan leaves. He pushed the fringe of black hair off his brow. It still was hot. But that was all right; he was used to it. What he was not used to, and what he could never get used to was that there was nothing to do. He wished that the tiger would come, though the thought made his scalp prickle. Then at least there would be some excitement.

No sparrow in its nest could have been more comfortable than the little village of Pinlebu in Upper Burma. Snug in the midst of soft, warm rice fields, it seemed borne on the back of the surrounding jungle. With the coming of the monsoon rains, Ko Shway knew, the jungle would steam and darken and the fields would turn to mud. The noise of parrots screaming and monkeys chattering, and the pungent, damp scent of the jungle would float out over the rice fields. Then the children of the village would drive the water buffaloes with the plow, and the rice would be planted, and the fields would be green.

But just now, under the blue, glittering sky, the sun's heat lay heavily like a blanket over the brown fields. No sound came from the village, and nothing moved. Everyone slept during the heat of the afternoon.

14

Ko Shway could see his house and beside it the house of his friend Tin Oo. Tin Oo and the others are probably snoring their lives away at home, he thought. He wondered if Tin Oo had heard the tiger calling. Well, maybe I'd better go and stir things up! He slid down into his tree house and pawed through his things. He decided to bring his clackers, and of course, his horn.

"A blast in Tin Oo's ear might do the trick," he said.

Laughing, he remembered that wonderful time when he had blown his horn in the ears of the water buffaloes, and they had stampeded through the village. The bellowing buffaloes had come rushing, wild-eyed, right down into the bazaar, upsetting trays of coconuts and piles of pineapples, and crashing through bananas hung in bunches from the low rafters. The water buffaloes belonged to U Gyi, and U Gyi had had to apologize to all the bazaar women, who were as ruffled as hens.

Maybe that's why he doesn't like me very much, Ko Shway thought. Well, I was younger then; I don't tease the buffaloes so much any more. Ko Shway hung his horn at his waist and skinned down the tree. He strode off across the rice fields, shaking his head and still laughing to himself. And when he noticed the water buffaloes looking balefully at him, he merely bowed in passing.

No one was outside as he entered the village, and he dodged behind a cluster of thatch houses so that he could sneak up on Tin Oo from behind his house. But Tin Oo saw him coming and flung a wicker ball at his head. Both of them dived for the ball, and after a scuffle in the dust, they collapsed and just lay there and laughed. Then they went to the well, arm in arm, splashed a little water, and sat down, leaning against the well. Ko Shway told Tin Oo about the tiger, making the story very big. He laughed when Tin Oo's eyes grew round and his mouth fell open, admiring and fearful. They talked for a while about the tiger, but decided it would never come where people were. Their minds turned to pondering what to do with the rest of the afternoon.

The trouble was, there was nothing going on in the village these days. Even the monastery school, which the boys of the village attended, was closed. The old monk, who had taught Buddhist scriptures and Burmese history (the only subjects they learned), had gone away to live out his last days in meditation, and no one had been sent to replace him.

"The last good thing was the Water Festival," Tin Oo said, and looked with a twinkle at Ko Shway.

They both laughed, thinking about it. The Water Festival! What a day that had been! Everyone throwing water, the girls dipping theirs so daintily from silver bowls, and running away when the boys came at them with bucketfuls, and giggling and laughing and falling down.

"Remember that water gun you made, Ko Shway?" Tin Oo said. "That was something!"

Ko Shway had made it of bamboo tubes and a piece of goatskin for a bag to hold the water. The water gushed out in great squirts when he squeezed the bag, catching everyone by surprise, and even the boys had run from him. And he had popped U Gyi in the eye by mistake, and U Gyi had spluttered and shook his fist.

"Yes, that was a good one, that Water Festival," Ko Shway said.

But now there would be nothing good happening until after the rainy season, when the first *pwe* would be performed. Then everyone would stay up all night watching the show, sitting on straw mats under the stars, sleeping sometimes, and eating fried grasshoppers and rice cakes and pickled tea leaves mixed with garlic and sesame seeds. But that would be months away. The boys slumped against the wall, idly prodding in the dust with their bare feet.

Suddenly Ko Shway sat up.

"Tin Oo," he cried, grabbing his friend's arm.

Tin Oo looked up hopefully.

Ko Shway spoke slowly, grandly. "Let's put on a pwe!" he said.

Tin Oo's eyebrows went up, and he looked at his friend. "Yes!" he exclaimed. "But, Ko Shway —how? For a pwe you need a stage and music and a beautiful girl to dance, and costumes and a buffoon."

"Sure you do," Ko Shway affirmed, laughing, "and we will have them. But let's take them one at a time. Now, a stage. . . ." And he scratched his head.

"I know!" Tin Oo said excitedly. "There's that old food stall in the field. Nobody uses it any more. We can pull off the sides for mats to put on the ground and use the platform for the stage."

"Good," said Ko Shway, getting up. "We have my clackers for music. You can be the orchestra, Tin Oo, and you can use my horn, too. And I"—he paused dramatically—"I will be the buffoon."

"Naturally." Tin Oo laughed as Ko Shway began to strut around, sticking out his stomach.

"I'll need a *gaung-baung*," he said, thinking of the round silk headdress men wore on special occasions. "Grandfather has a peacock-blue one; I'll get that. And I'll need a silk longyi to wear. Tin Oo," he said with a mischievous grin, "do you think your father would mind if we borrow his emerald-green longyi. . . . I mean, if he doesn't know about it till afterward?"

"Oh, Ko Shway!" his friend gasped, appalled. But it was the perfect thing, so he said, "All right."

"We had better borrow your mother's blue one while we're at it," Ko Shway said to the shocked Tin Oo, adding coolly, "for the dancing girl."

"What dancing girl?" Tin Oo was skeptical.

"Never mind. I'll tell you later. I have an idea. Come on, Tin Oo," he said, clapping his friend on the back. "Let's go get the things." And off they went.

Chapter 2

The boys sneaked into Tin Oo's house, where everyone was still napping. Tin Oo quietly raised the lid of the red lacquer chest which held his parents' best longyis.

"Oh, Ko Shway, maybe we shouldn't—" Tin Oo giggled nervously, backing away from the chest and the carefully folded lengths of silk. But Ko Shway said, "Shh," and hurriedly hauled out the longyis.

Under the longyis was a box of cheroot cigars, each one about the size of a small ear of corn. Ko Shway decided to bring these, too, to add to the festivities. They crept out again, and once outside, ran to the field. Tin Oo pulled down the bamboo-strip sides of the stall and began to arrange them invitingly on the ground in front of it.

"Back in a minute. I'm going to get the danc-ing girl," Ko Shway said. Laughing at Tin Oo's puzzled look, he bounded off across the field.

"First the gaung-baung," he said to himself as he reached his house.

His grandfather also had a lacquer chest, and in it Ko Shway found the gaung-baung. But he found something else, too. One time he had made a mask with the puffy face and popping eyes and sour expression of U Gyi. But his grandfather had taken it away from him—and here it was.

"The perfect thing!" Ko Shway exclaimed, and he put it on.

Outside again, he ran across his yard to where his grandfather's old nanny goat was standing, staring blankly. Pulling on the end of her rope, he led her out and across the field.

"Look, Tin Oo," he shouted, and began to prance.

Tin Oo's laughter rang out. "Oh, Ko Shway, you look exactly like U Gyi!"

"U Tin Oo," Ko Shway said, with an exagger-ated bow, indicating the goat, "permit me to in-

troduce Ma Pyo, the most beautiful, the most
sought after, the most elegant dancer in all
Burma."

Tin Oo bowed and said, giggling, "Charmed."
The nanny goat said, "Nehhh."

Ko Shway addressed the nanny goat. "Beautiful
Ma Pyo, now you must dress for the pwe." He
grabbed up the blue longyi. And though Ma Pyo

went on saying "Nehhh" and tried to sit down, the boys managed to wrestle her into the costume.

Then Ko Shway put on the emerald-green longyi, fixing all the extra lengths of silk across his stomach to build it out in fat folds. It dragged a little on the ground, but he was ready. Tin Oo had begun to bang the clackers and stamp with his feet.

While all this was going on, the village began to awaken. Tin Oo's little sister Mi Mi came out to play with her friend Chit Chit, the young daughter of U Gyi. The two little girls were having a tea party for their dolls in the dusty courtyard outside Tin Oo's house. But the sounds of the clacker and the stamping and the protests of Ma Pyo made them look up, and they decided to go and see.

When Ko Shway saw them standing shyly at the edge of the field, hesitant to come forward, he called out, "Come one, come all—the pwe is about to begin."

The little girls just stood there, taken aback by the mask and the strangeness. Tin Oo strode over to them, and giving his little sister a prod, started

24

them forward. Then he and Ko Shway ushered them to the mats and pushed them down. They sat there, clutching their dolls and staring up at the boys, and Chit Chit looked as if she were going to cry.

So Ko Shway lifted his mask for a moment and said, "See, Chit Chit, it's only me. We're having a pwe. You'd like that, wouldn't you?" And, looking around for something to cheer the girls up, he saw the cheroot cigars.

"Chit Chit," he said, "have you ever seen a pwe?" She shook her head solemnly.

"No? Too young, I guess." Ko Shway nodded; he looked very sympathetic.

"Well, you see, Chit Chit, at a pwe all the ladies smoke cheroots. That's how you can tell they are ladies. So it would be a very nice thing if you and Mi Mi would be the ladies at our pwe, and smoke cheroots." And, temptingly, he held one out to each.

Tin Oo took matches from the cheroot box and squatted down beside the girls, nodding in a friendly way. Ko Shway said, "I'll show you

how," and putting a cigar in his mouth, he beck-
oned Tin Oo to light it. When it was burning
brightly, and he had puffed out a cloud of smoke,
he gave it to Chit Chit and prepared one for Mi
Mi.

The little girls, finally won over by all the attention and kindness, tried hard to make smoke,
copying Ko Shway, making a little round *O* and
drawing in on the end of their big cheroots.

"Fine!" said Ko Shway, leaping up. "Now we
can begin."

Ma Pyo, meanwhile, tied to a post on the platform, paid no attention and stood staring out at
nothing.

"She's waiting for her cue," Ko Shway said. He
handed Tin Oo the horn, and the boys leapt up
onto the stage.

First Ko Shway pranced and postured and posed
in a clumsy dance that was something like the
antics of a real pwe buffoon and something like
the paunchy strut of U Gyi. Tin Oo clacked and
stamped. Then Ko Shway introduced Ma Pyo to
the small audience, who sat enthralled, peering

through the smoke. And Tin Oo helped the introduction along. He took a deep breath and, holding the horn to his mouth, sent forth a mighty blast.

Now, Ma Pyo had not heard that horn since the day the water buffaloes had stampeded through the village. But she had not forgotten.

Flinging her hindquarters into the air, she tried to make her exit. But, because she was tied, she landed instead on her head, her costume flying up over her ears. She leapt up and danced on her hind legs, her forelegs paddling air, her head invisible beneath the layers of silk.

The little girls laughed and cheered and waved their cigars, and Tin Oo blew again and again on the horn. Ko Shway danced around and around Ma Pyo.

Just at this time U Gyi was taking his afternoon walk in the village, accompanied by two of his friends. And when the din reached them, they were, of course, curious to know what was going on. So they hurried to the field. And this is what they saw: a goat dancing in a blue silk longyi; an

27

orchestra of one making a noise like ten; and a small, prancing buffoon dancing about in a fat and silly way.

U Gyi's friends laughed and laughed. "It's you, U Gyi!" they said. "Exactly!" "And," one of them added, choking with laughter, "isn't that

your daughter—there in the smoke?" U Gyi just
stared and stared, popeyed.

Tin Oo was the first to see U Gyi, and the music
stopped with a little bleat. Ma Pyo came out from
under her costume and looked about, dazed. But
Ko Shway continued his dance in full swing. As

29

he made a sweeping turn, his eye fell on U Gyi, standing there, taking it all in.

Tin Oo grabbed Ko Shway's arm and started to run. But Ko Shway, taking too big a step, tripped over his longyi and fell against Tin Oo.

Just then, Ma Pyo gathered herself for one last desperate leap and plunged off the stage, snapping her tether. Tin Oo jumped to stop her, but she landed on her back among the little girls, scattering them and their dolls and their cigars. Ma Pyo scrambled to her feet, tore off her costume with her teeth, trampled it in the dust, and was gone.

Now U Gyi came lumbering toward the boys, his fist in the air. But Chit Chit, wailing loudly, held up her arms to him. He scooped her up, but she leaned down over his arm, sobbing, "Please, my dolly, too." He bent heavily to gather up the doll.

Mi Mi said, "I don't feel very well." She looked rather green, and so did Chit Chit.

U Gyi's friends were picking up the cigars; not wanting to interfere, they stood at one side smoking them, very much amused. Seeing their chance,

Ko Shway and Tin Oo scrambled off the back of the platform and ran.

U Gyi's anger at last broke out. "Ko Shway," he roared, and swung toward the platform. But the stage was empty. The performers had departed. Nothing remained but a piece of rope and a simpering paper mask.

The hullabaloo lasted for a week. Everyone was talking about the pwe. U Gyi came and yelled at Ko Shway's grandfather, and Ko Shway was sorry because his grandfather was sad. "Some day that boy will go too far!" U Gyi told several people. But they laughed and said no real damage had been done. The little girls had been up and around the next day, none the worse. Tin Oo and Ko Shway had been sternly lectured, and Ko Shway and his grandfather had presented a new longyi to Tin Oo's mother.

And it really was funny, Ko Shway thought. Whenever U Gyi walked in the village, children giggled and whispered among themselves. Women smiled broadly at him, and his friends grinned and offered him cheroots. Ko Shway knew that U Gyi's dignity was gone and that U Gyi could not look anyone in the eye until he got it back.

U Gyi was a pompous man. But, though Ko Shway did not realize it, he was also a generous one. The water buffaloes belonged to him, and he let everyone use them for the plowing. He had built the pagoda and the town hall. The villagers depended on him for almost everything; but he had an air of self-importance which made them feel small. Perhaps that is why they were glad for a chance to laugh at him.

A week after the pwe, U Gyi made a speech on the steps in front of the town hall. Ko Shway and Tin Oo, coming from the tree house, stood at the back of the crowd of villagers and listened as U Gyi cleared his throat loudly and began:

"As you know, Pinlebu village is without a school. We do not know when the monastery school will open again. So I have arranged for a teacher to come to our village. She is willing to teach all of our children, not just the boys."

A clamor of surprise broke out. *She!* A woman

teacher—that was something new! And a teacher for all the children! It would be the first time in Pinlebu village that the girls would go to school.

Ko Shway and Tin Oo looked at each other. "What do you think, Ko Shway?" Tin Oo whispered. But U Gyi was raising his arms to quiet the crowd.

"Daw Ma Ma is the name of the teacher. She comes tomorrow from Mandalay." His satisfied smile changed to a grimace, and he glowered for a moment at Ko Shway's grandfather, who was leaning on a stick at the front of the crowd. "Let us hope she will bring some much-needed discipline into the lives of our young people."

"One thing more," U Gyi went on. "I do not want to alarm you. You have all heard reports that there is a tiger in the vicinity. Of course, I do not believe these rumors. In any case, he would not come near the village. But you should not let your children go into the jungle. They will be much better off in school."

"And," his voice rasped, "perhaps now we will have some peace and quiet in this village!" He

33

glared again at Ko Shway's grandfather and stomped down the steps.

The villagers buzzed with excitement. As they walked through the bazaar, dropping off in small groups at the teahouse, all they could talk about was the coming of the teacher.

Ko Shway and Tin Oo walked toward the tree house, and Ko Shway, looking over his shoulder to see that no one was watching, mimicked in a sour voice, "Perhaps now we will have some peace and quiet in this village!"

Tin Oo was silent. Ko Shway went on. "U Gyi meant us. He thinks we're troublemakers. We were just having fun—trying to find something to do." He added defiantly, "Going to school isn't going to change that."

"Don't you want to go to school, Ko Shway?" Tin Oo asked, surprised at his friend's anger. "You liked monastery school."

"I liked history. I liked learning about the kings of Burma. What does an old woman know about the kings of Burma?"

Ko Shway strode ahead of his friend and, arriving at the banyan tree, swung himself up and began to climb. Tin Oo, puffing as he climbed behind him up the tree, said, "But it's something to do! And it might be fun."

"She might be mean, like U Gyi," Ko Shway answered crossly over his shoulder. "That wouldn't be fun."

In the tree house, Ko Shway began to whittle on a piece of wood. He glanced at his friend, who sat sadly staring at his feet.

"Oh, well," Ko Shway said, relenting. "Maybe it will be fun. Cheer up, Tin Oo." He smiled and gave Tin Oo a friendly push. "You know what!" he suddenly cried, and his eyes sparkled. "Maybe she will have books!"

Daw Ma Ma arrived the next afternoon, hot and dusty from the long drive over bumpy roads in a rattly old jeep. When she climbed out, all smiling and pleasant, the children bunched around her like grapes on a stem. But U Gyi bustled up and plucked off the children, telling them they could stare at her as much as they liked on the first day

of school, but that now he would be in charge.

"She's young!" Ko Shway whispered to Tin Oo.

"And pretty!" Tin Oo replied.

U Gyi bowed and greeted Daw Ma Ma respectfully. He introduced a number of villagers, who bowed politely.

"And who are these children?" Daw Ma Ma

asked, smiling at Ko Shway, Tin Oo, and the others, who grinned back.

Chit Chit was clinging to her father's longyi and peeking out from behind him. U Gyi disengaged Chit Chit and presented her to Daw Ma Ma.

"Daw Ma Ma," he said proudly, "this is my daughter, Chit Chit. And these are two of the older boys." Tin Oo and Ko Shway stepped forward eagerly. "This is Tin Oo, the son of U Nanda. And this," U Gyi said, looking as if he smelled something unpleasant, "is Ko Shway." He leaned close to Daw Ma Ma and with a frozen smile confided, "Ko Shway is the village clown."

Ko Shway could feel the top of his head turning hot and prickly, but he was about to bow when U Gyi turned Daw Ma Ma's attention to the other children crowding in to be introduced.

"Let's go," Ko Shway said urgently to Tin Oo, and the boys edged out of the crowd. They walked in silence for a while. Then, "What are you thinking about, Ko Shway?" Tin Oo asked his friend.

But Ko Shway just smiled mysteriously and said, "Wait and see."

Chapter 3

It was the first day of school, and to Ko Shway
this seemed very odd indeed. The monastery
school had never started before the first rains.
But this new teacher from Mandalay had some
peculiar ideas. Everyone had been surprised when
Daw Ma Ma had said, "No, we cannot wait for
the rains. The rains will be late this year, but
school will not. If we are to learn, we must
begin."

U Gyi went busily about the village cautioning
everyone to be in his place when the teacher arrived. And so all the children of the village, wear-
ing fresh new longyis, dutifully trooped off to
school in the heat of the morning.

"Come on, Ko Shway," Tin Oo called as the
children passed his house. Ko Shway joined them,

draping his arm over the shoulder of his best friend, all of them laughing and joking and complaining about the heat and wondering about the new teacher and school.

Everyone went into the schoolhouse to wait for the teacher—everyone, that is, except Ko Shway. He winked, waved them a cheery good-by, and ducked around behind the school. He had a plan of his own.

He rummaged around under a lantana bush until he felt with his hands the lumpy thing he was seeking. Chuckling to himself, he carefully lifted it out and sat down with it balanced on his knees. He stripped away the banana leaves, and there, grimacing at him, was his tiger's head.

He looked it over carefully, considering. "Yes, tiger, you will do," he said. Holding it tightly against his chest, he crept along under the bushes beside the school. When he had rounded the corner, he crouched low. And there he waited, very, very quietly. But his heart was pounding loudly, and he almost burst out laughing as he wondered if that city teacher had ever in her life seen a tiger.

At last Daw Ma Ma came walking briskly along near the bazaar on the other side of the open field in front of the school.

Though it was not yet nine o'clock, the sun beat its way through the tall trees, and the warm dust of the road swirled and filtered through her sandals. The food-sellers in the bazaar had lowered their bamboo awnings to protect the food and themselves from the hot sun and the puffs of dust sweeping down the main street of the village. Several women, hurrying to the bazaar with baskets of food on their heads, greeted her respectfully.

Ko Shway saw Daw Ma Ma return their greeting and hurry on, past the bazaar and across the field. She was looking at the one-room building. It had a thatched roof and bamboo sides for protection from the wind and rain, and the earth was the floor.

She was walking faster now, her books held firmly in her arms. When she was only a few yards from the school and the bushes where Ko Shway was hidden, Daw Ma Ma paused for a moment.

She patted her hair and smoothed her longyi. As she took a step forward, Ko Shway gave a low growl—a deep animal growl. Daw Ma Ma turned and stared at the bushes. Ko Shway crouched in silence. After a moment she started toward the school again, and again he growled. This time she walked right over to the bushes. As her face peered through the leaves, Ko Shway lunged forward with a deafening roar, thrusting the tiger head right at her.

"Eee!" she shrieked. "Tiger!" she screamed. And she jumped back, dropped her books, and covered her head. Suddenly she cried, "Oh, dear, the children!" And she began to run toward the schoolroom, yelling "Oh!" and "Tiger!" all the way.

In the schoolroom the children, who had seen the teacher approaching through the field, had all been sitting properly at their tables. But when they heard the commotion, some of the bigger boys leapt up and saw Daw Ma Ma rushing toward the school, waving her arms and shouting "Tiger!" And behind Daw Ma Ma was a tiger's

head rolling in the dust. And behind the tiger's head was Ko Shway, standing with his legs apart and his hands on his hips, his head thrown back and a smile like the smile of the Cheshire cat all over his face.

Daw Ma Ma burst into the room. "Down, quickly," she cried, running along the rows of children. "Everybody under the tables! You,

there, help the little ones!'' Then, as they all
began to scramble under the tables, she picked up
a bamboo pole and moved cautiously to the doorway.

But where was the tiger? And what was that
child doing outside? And what was that lumpy
thing he was carrying?

At last Daw Ma Ma understood. ''So that's it,''

she said, and Ko Shway saw her smile slightly. He
stood there, grinning at her from a safe distance,
balancing the tiger's head on one hip and watching
her with interest. She looked as if she wanted to
thwack him with the bamboo pole, but instead
she put it carefully down and walked to where her
books were scattered on the ground.

Ko Shway watched her picking them up one by
one, occasionally glancing at him, as if inviting
him to help her. She looked small and shaken, and
he felt a little sorry that he had frightened her.
Something in her look let him know that if he
helped her now it would be all right. He took a
step forward. But suddenly a sound drew his attention to the schoolroom; there were the children all peering out under the bamboo shades,
laughing and pointing. Ko Shway bowed, grinned,
and turning, bounded off into the field.

Ko Shway zigzagged across the field and worked
his way back behind the building. He reached his
hand to the bamboo screen, very quietly parted

the slats, and peeked in. He was behind Daw Ma Ma.

In back of each row of benches stood a row of boys and girls. All were waiting uncertainly, and Mi Mi and Chit Chit in the front row, frightened by Ko Shway's tiger and Daw Ma Ma's newness, had begun to cry.

"All right, class, sit down," Daw Ma Ma said firmly. She walked over to the girls in the front row. "Do not be afraid. I am not a tiger, and I will not roar at you, nor bite you. Stop crying." She returned to the platform in the front of the room and sat down at the table.

"Now we shall begin," she said. "You know that my name is Daw Ma Ma, but I do not know all your names. Each pupil will stand and say his name. I will write it on this chart here, and each day when you come to school you will sit in the seat you are sitting in today. That way I shall learn your names quickly. Do you understand?"

Heads nodded, and each child stood shyly to give his name and quickly sat down again. There was a pause in the name-telling, and Daw Ma Ma looked up. "Tin Oo," she said. "Who is after Tin Oo?"

Tin Oo, at the back of the room with the other big boys, scrambled to his feet and blurted, "No one is after me, teacher. The place beside me is empty."

Daw Ma Ma addressed the class. "Who has not come to school today?" she asked. But before they could answer, Ko Shway gave a snicker and quickly covered his mouth with his hand. The slats clicked together. Daw Ma Ma glanced behind her, and again she smiled slightly.

"The boy who plays tiger—what is his name?" she asked gently, and looked at Chit Chit.

Chit Chit stood shyly and said, "His name is Ko Shway. And . . . and. . . ." She began crying again. "And there really are tigers in the jungle," she stammered through her tears.

Her crying set off the whole front row. And to the little girls' wails were soon added the hoots and jeers of the older boys. Daw Ma Ma rapped her pencil sharply on the table.

"A schoolroom is no place for hooting and jeering," she said. "Nor is it a place for crying. And we will have no more of it. We have come here to learn, and that is what we will do."

Daw Ma Ma picked up a bulging folder and opened it. "Today I shall give each of you a picture to look at."

Ko Shway was still crouching outside the window. He couldn't see, but he didn't dare open the slats again.

Daw Ma Ma held up a colored picture of a huge golden pagoda gleaming in the sunlight. Monks in saffron robes and people carrying flowers and candles strolled on the many terraces of the pagoda.

The children stared with open mouths at the picture, then began to murmur to one another. Ko Shway, hearing the excitement, tried desperately to see through the blinds without touching them. He couldn't see a thing!

The children had never seen such a picture before—with gold and saffron and red, and a pagoda larger than any they could have imagined. It could only be the Shwe Dagon Pagoda, the jewel of Burma, in the far-off city of Rangoon.

47

Daw Ma Ma smiled and gave the picture to Chit Chit, who was now beaming. The teacher passed through the rows of children, giving to each a picture from her folder. The room hummed with "Oh" and "Ah" and "Look!"

Finally Daw Ma Ma clapped her hands. "Now, children," she said, "each one will show his picture. He will tell what he sees, and then I will tell you things about the picture you probably do not know. This way we will learn about our country. Come, Chit Chit, we will start with you."

And so the first lessons began.

But Ko Shway, who could not see the pictures, slumped down beside the building, leaning his back against it and waiting for the day to be over. On the whole, he thought, the joke had been a success. It was funny when the teacher screamed and ran. Except . . . except, he hadn't expected it would turn out quite like that. He hadn't expected she would take it so seriously. She was really frightened, he thought, with a little pang of guilt. And he hadn't expected to be missing school and everything. "Just waiting isn't any fun," he said to himself.

48

At last he heard the scrunch of benches being moved; and the children, laughing and talking, poured out of the schoolhouse.

"Well, finally," he said a little crossly, and crawled to peer around the corner looking for Tin Oo.

But Tin Oo came out with Daw Ma Ma. "May I walk with you, teacher?" he was saying politely.

"He's forgotten about me!" Ko Shway was indignant. His friend had forgotten him! A strange mixture of disappointment and distress and anger filled him, and not really wanting to, Ko Shway followed the pair at a distance.

Chapter 4

Perhaps Ko Shway would have felt less forgotten if he had known what Daw Ma Ma and Tin Oo were talking about.

They walked in comfortable silence for a few moments, and then Tin Oo said, "Those pictures, teacher. They are beautiful. Where did you get them?"

Daw Ma Ma smiled. "From magazines, from books, from everywhere. I have collected them for a long time. Friends from all over the world send me pictures."

"We have never seen such pictures. There are hardly any magazines or books in our village. But Ko Shway says. . . ." He paused.

"Yes," she questioned. "What does Ko Shway say?"

"Well, teacher," Tin Oo stuttered, "Ko Shway says that he will have books and pictures some day."

"Oh?" Daw Ma Ma was surprised. "Tell me more about Ko Shway."

"Teacher, Ko Shway is not really a bad boy. He is my friend, and he is very clever. But sometimes there's nothing to do, and, well—he does like to play tricks on people. Not to hurt them, really; just to scare them a little or just to see what will happen."

"It is not always wise to do things 'just to see what will happen,'" said Daw Ma Ma. "Sometimes what happens is not at all what we expect. But thank you for telling me about your friend. And now, could you take me to Ko Shway's house? I would like to speak with his parents."

"Oh," said Tin Oo, taken by surprise. "Ko Shway lives with his grandfather. Their house is next to mine. We can go by this path here."

They were about to turn off into a narrow path when U Gyi came hurrying toward them, waving his arms and calling to Daw Ma Ma.

"Come, teacher, this way," urged Tin Oo, steering her into the path. "See. That house there with the goat tied to the fence."

But it was no use. U Gyi was running now and shouting at the top of his lungs. He came up to them, red of face and short of breath, his roly-poly body heaving.

"Daw Ma Ma! Daw Ma Ma!" he gasped. "I must speak to you! My daughter has told me what happened at school today. That boy! That Ko Shway!" He looked distastefully at Tin Oo. "You may leave us, Tin Oo. I wish to speak to Daw Ma Ma in private."

"Thank you again, Tin Oo," she said, smiling at him and gently collecting her books. Then she turned her attention to U Gyi. Tin Oo, with a worried glance over his shoulder, went slowly down the path.

Ko Shway, following behind, watched Tin Oo walking with the teacher, carrying her books, talking with her intently. Other children waved to him and called out as he passed. But nobody said a word about the tiger joke. They were too busy showing each other their pictures.

Feeling that somehow everything had gone wrong, Ko Shway saw U Gyi rush up to Daw Ma Ma. He saw her greet him politely and saw U Gyi wave Tin Oo away. Ko Shway slipped behind a gardenia tree to wait for his friend. Wait, wait, wait, that's all I do, he thought.

Watching his friend walk slowly toward him, he called out testily, "Hurry up, Tin Oo!" He had to know whether the joke was really a success.

"Well, ye-e-es," Tin Oo said, not very convincingly. "But Ko Shway, you should see the pictures Daw Ma Ma gave us," he went on in a voice filled with excitement. "Look, here's mine!" And he proudly displayed his picture of elephants hauling teak logs.

Ko Shway took the picture in his hands and whistled admiringly. The boys sat down under the gardenia tree, and Ko Shway felt more and more troubled as Tin Oo told him all that he had missed at school and about Daw Ma Ma and the pictures, finishing off with, "Actually, Ko Shway,

53

I don't think you should have done that, you
know, with the tiger. Daw Ma Ma didn't like it.
She's . . . she's at your house now, I think, talking
to your grandfather."

"At my house!" Ko Shway gasped.

They sat for a while in worried silence. Then
Ko Shway got up. "Tin Oo," he said, "I have
made a mistake. A whopper! I wish—" he started,

but it was too late for wishing. Then he said resolutely, "I am going home."

"I know why you have come, Daw Ma Ma. Ko Shway has set the whole village talking. Again!" Ko Shway's grandfather leaned forward earnestly. "It is because he has no parents to help him, I think," the old man said. "When his mother died three years ago, his father went to live in the monastery."

Daw Ma Ma had found the old man sitting on a mat in front of his house, drinking tea. She had greeted him politely, using the word *uncle,* a greeting reserved for old and respected men. U San Paw had invited her to sit with him, served her some tea, and without any further exchange of politenesses, had abruptly begun to talk about Ko Shway.

He went on. "I love my grandson dearly. But I am an old man, not suited to the task of bringing up such an energetic boy."

He sighed, and then looked squarely at Daw Ma Ma. "But Ko Shway is not a cruel boy, nor a wicked one. He is bright, and clever with his hands, and I had hoped with the coming of a proper teacher to Pinlebu village, the boy might—"

He looked away from Daw Ma Ma and said sadly, "But he has made a poor beginning, hasn't he, young lady?"

At that moment Ko Shway came through the gate and stood contritely before them.

"Good evening, Grandfather," he said, and then, almost whispering, "Good evening, teacher."

There was an awkward silence. Ko Shway cleared his throat. "Grandfather, I—" he began. He wanted to say he was sorry, quickly, and be done with it. But his grandfather interrupted him.

"I suppose you are sorry," he said. "You usually are. And that is good. I am aware, Ko Shway, that you do not intend the damage you cause. But I wonder if you are aware of just how serious a problem you might have made for the village. Quite apart from the distress you caused Daw Ma

Ma, what do you think would have happened if the rumor of tiger—started by you—had swept through the village. What would have happened, eh?"

"Well—everyone would have been awfully scared," Ko Shway said; but he did not find the prospect funny. Something in his grandfather's tone prevented that. He thought of the tiger whose distant call he had heard; how foolish his joke seemed now. "But, Grandfather," he said, "no tiger has come to Pinlebu village for years!"

"Oh. So," his grandfather said very sternly. "And what do you know about 'tigers' and 'years'? How many years have you been in Pinlebu village?" He turned to Daw Ma Ma. "My grandson thinks that because the tiger is his birthsign, he knows all about the beast."

"No, Grandfather, but—" He stopped when he saw an angry flash in his grandfather's eye.

"Boy, you know nothing about tigers!"

"I know they don't harm *people!*" Ko Shway blurted, stung by his grandfather's harsh tone. "Only if they're hurt or hungry or scared."

"And how do you know," his grandfather said witheringly, "when they are hurt or hungry or scared?"

"Oh," said Ko Shway in a small voice. He hadn't thought of that.

His grandfather's look was more kindly now. "You were only a baby, Ko Shway, the last time," he said. "It was a time when the jungle animals were very hungry and had begun to come closer and closer to the villages for food. They were hungry because the monsoon rains were late—*as they are this year*," he said slowly and meaningfully.

"Oh, Grandfather," Ko Shway said, his eyes getting big. "What happened?"

"Well, what happened was," his grandfather said dryly, "that some villages lost their pigs and their goats; and at Pinlebu village we lost our only water buffalo. Fortunately, no people were killed. But after that, it was not until U Gyi came and brought his water buffaloes that the people could give up plowing by hand."

Ko Shway hung his head. He mumbled, "I'm

sorry. I didn't know. I didn't think." He looked up with a worried frown.

"Well," his grandfather said, and cleared his throat. "Now, apologize to your teacher."

So Ko Shway bent before her and said, his voice trembling, "Teacher, I am so sorry. I really am."

She replied, "Ko Shway, we have both learned a lesson from U San Paw. So some good came out of it, didn't it? Now I only regret that you missed school today."

"So do I!" said Ko Shway, and he looked with longing at the folder of pictures beside her.

Daw Ma Ma said with a twinkle, "But tell me one thing, Ko Shway. Where did you get that tiger's head? It looked so real!"

Ko Shway smiled and said eagerly, "Well, you see, teacher, I studied tigers in a book of U Gyi's. U Gyi has books," he explained. "Then, I made one."

"My grandson makes all kinds of things, Daw Ma Ma."

"You do, too, Grandfather. My grandfather is a potter," he said proudly to Daw Ma Ma. "And so

60

was my father before—" He stopped abruptly and looked at U San Paw.

"Let us go into the house," his grandfather said. "Daw Ma Ma, we would be most honored if you would join us for supper."

Daw Ma Ma accepted with pleasure.

"I'll carry your folder for you, teacher," Ko Shway said, bending quickly and taking it into his hands.

Ko Shway's house was much like all village houses in Pinlebu. Straw mats covered the floor, and a wide, low platform for eating and sitting and sleeping took up most of the room. A lacquer chest and covered grass baskets lined the bamboo walls. On a high narrow shelf in one corner of the room sat a statue of the Buddha, lit by candles and set off on either side by vases of fresh flowers.

As U San Paw ushered Daw Ma Ma to the platform, fussing a bit to make her comfortable, Tin Oo appeared in the doorway. He was carrying two large bowls.

"Come in, Tin Oo," said U San Paw, and turning to Daw Ma Ma, he explained, "Tin Oo's mother has been kind enough to prepare our supper for us. She has been taking care of us since Ko Shway's mother died."

Ko Shway set a short, round table in the middle of the platform and helped Tin Oo arrange the bowls of glistening yellow curry and soft, white rice. The fragrance of cinnamon and bay and saffron and chicken made them all suddenly quite hungry.

Tin Oo exchanged a glance with Ko Shway and gave him a nudge with his elbow. Ko Shway said, "Grandfather, please may Tin Oo stay for supper?" And, receiving a smile and a nod, they were quickly seated, cross-legged, at the table.

Daw Ma Ma, as the guest, began. Dipping the fingers of one hand delicately into the rice, she made a little ball and then dipped this into the curry. Soon all were eating—dipping and munching and chattering merrily.

After supper Daw Ma Ma picked up her folder. "Now, what would be a good picture for the boy who plays tiger?" And she began to look through the pictures, spreading them out on the platform.

Ko Shway, who had been afraid this moment would never come, watched eagerly over her shoulder.

"Why don't you look through the pictures and decide," she said.

Ko Shway began very carefully to inspect the pictures. Tin Oo tried to help, saying, "How about this one?" and, "That's a good one!" to every picture that met his eye.

But Ko Shway could not decide. He could not find the one, the exact one he had been hoping for. Finally he said, "They are beautiful pictures, teacher. But—"

"But what, Ko Shway?"

"But," he went on all in a rush, "I was looking, teacher, for a picture of King Anawrahta leading his armies against his enemies."

"That you will not find, Ko Shway. You see," Daw Ma Ma explained, "King Anawrahta lived a very long time ago, and there were no photographs in those days. But I do have something— let me see—" She began searching through the pictures. "I have a picture of a puppet show, and one of the puppets is King Anawrahta. Yes, here it is." And she held it up.

The puppets were quite large, carved from wood, and splendidly dressed in silk; and the tallest wore a golden crown. Ko Shway took the picture from Daw Ma Ma and gazed at it with a sigh of satisfaction.

"Yes, teacher," he finally said, looking up and smiling broadly. "This is the one!"

"Good. Then it's settled," Daw Ma Ma said. "And now, I must leave."

The boys jumped up and offered to walk with Daw Ma Ma. She said good-by and thanked U San Paw, and they went out into the clear Burmese evening.

Ko Shway, carrying the folder, walked proudly beside his teacher.

It was cooler now, and the trees and houses of the village looked black against the deepened blue of the sky. The scent of gardenia trees was sweet around them, and the tiny yellow puffballs of the mimosa blew about them on the gentle breeze.

U San Paw stood in the doorway of his house. He gazed out toward the dark jungle, and then up into the sky. The old man's look went deep as he tried to fathom that blue mystery. How soon, how soon would it rain?

And in the jungle, the animals were growing hungrier and hungrier . . . .

Chapter 5

The rice fields baked and cracked under the scorching sun. The water buffaloes had to look hard for little patches of mud to keep damp in. In the village there was no work to be done— although the bazaar was open in the mornings and the evenings. People sat around smoking cheroots, talking lazily, and just waiting for the rains.

Not many people ventured into the jungle these days. There was plenty of water, still, in the deeper wells, though most of the jungle ponds and streams were dry, and the crackling jungle foliage shriveled more each day. The rice harvest had been good the year before, so there was enough food. But no visitors or merchants came through the jungle from neighboring villages, and the people had a lonely, cutoff feeling.

"It's like being under siege!" Ko Shway said to his friend.

People began to be nervous and irritable. They spoke crossly to each other, and the least disagreement flared into an argument.

The main problem was a shortage of wood for cooking-fires. It was the children's job to gather wood in the jungle. But U Gyi's rule that no children should go into the jungle had put a stop to that. And U Gyi was very firm about this.

Ko Shway did not hear the tiger again, but he thought about it often.

Ko Shway and the other school children were luckier than the grownups. At least they had something to do. Ko Shway sat in his place at the back of the room, sometimes listening intently, sometimes chiming in. When his turn came to talk about his picture, he told not only what was in the picture, but also what he imagined about the adventures of King Anawrahta. And Daw Ma Ma told Ko Shway the names of the king's generals and the enemies' generals and much more he hadn't known.

Ko Shway looked at his picture with new interest, and he spent long hours pouring over a book about puppets which Daw Ma Ma had given him. He discovered that puppet-making was an ancient art in Burma, an art passed on from father to son, each generation carefully guarding its secrets. There were few puppet-makers left in the country, but the most famous, Ba Min, still practiced his art in Mandalay.

One day after school, Daw Ma Ma asked Ko Shway to stay in his seat. As he watched the other children leave, Ko Shway's mind flitted back through the day. For once he couldn't think of anything he had done wrong. When Daw Ma Ma called him, he stood uncertainly in front of her desk.

"This is a hard time for the village, Ko Shway," she began. "Even the children are becoming nervous. Chit Chit would cry if you said 'Boo' to her."

"I know," Ko Shway grinned. "I said 'Boo' to her, and she did cry!"

Daw Ma Ma smiled wearily. "Ko Shway, Ko

Shway," she murmured, shaking her head. She looked tired.

She spoke again. "Perhaps there is something we can do to help the village."

"What can we do? We don't know how to bring the rain!"

"No, of course not," Daw Ma Ma answered. "But I have been thinking. Perhaps we could put on a puppet show or a play—something to entertain the village and take their thoughts away from the trouble."

"A puppet show!" Ko Shway shouted. Then, his excitement fading, "But we do not have a puppet-maker."

Suddenly Ko Shway knew why Daw Ma Ma had asked him to wait after school.

"Teacher," he said, "you want *me* to make the puppets? Me!" He looked at her face to read her thoughts, not quite trusting his own.

"Well, Ko Shway, could you? You have been reading my book about Ba Min, the great puppet master. Could you try?"

A thousand thoughts rushed through Ko

Shway's head. The wood must be just right, and he needed the proper tools. Yes, his collection of knives would do for the carving. It would take hours and hours of patient carving. String—where would he get the string? But never mind, one of the bazaar ladies would surely give it to him. Tin Oo could make the stage, and yes—Chit Chit and the other girls could sew the costumes.

"Well, Ko Shway?"

Ko Shway looked down into the eyes of his teacher. "Yes, teacher," he said, "I will make the puppets. I will make King Anawrahta conquering his enemies. But I will not come to school any more until they are made!" And he dashed out of the schoolroom before Daw Ma Ma had a chance to protest.

In his tree house Ko Shway sat cross-legged, an open book in his lap. Around him lay his few tools, several balls of kite string, and a number of pieces of soft wood, some already carved in the shape of legs and arms. Tacked to the grass wall was the picture of the puppets given him by Daw Ma Ma.

His absorbed gaze took in each detail of the picture. In the center was King Anawrahta, very noble-looking, very proud. He was taller than the two ministers of state behind him, probably about three feet tall, Ko Shway judged. The carving of his features was precise and intricate. I will need hard wood for the face, Ko Shway thought.

It was difficult to determine how the joints in the neck, shoulders, and knees were constructed, because the rich, jeweled robes covered them. The book on his lap did not hold the answers either, he discovered, leafing through the pages he now knew by heart. I can figure that out, though, he thought.

The other figures in the picture were an elephant, a monkey, and a parrot. These, he knew, represented the animal kingdom, which, like the human subjects, was loyal to the king. Those would be easy; they would not have to look like someone special. But King Anawrahta—how to show in his face that he was a great leader? I will finish the others first, Ko Shway decided, for practice. And then, perhaps, my hands will know enough to form the king.

Now Ko Shway was no longer alone in his tree house. Hanging from the branches that formed the ceiling were the puppets. Their arms and legs caught at angles by the strings, they seemed arrested in strange poses, as if they had been dancing and suddenly the music had stopped. Even the elephant, one large foot raised, seemed part of the dance.

But at Ko Shway's feet lay the headless body of King Anawrahta. Ko Shway looked at it and gave it a rough push with his foot. How could he carve the head when he did not have the right wood?

"I need teak," he said aloud. But there was no teak.

The puppets, moving slightly on their strings, seemed to be staring at him, mocking him. He glared at one and then another of these creatures he had made.

"Stop staring," he shouted, and grabbing up his grandfather's ax, he climbed down the banyan tree.

He would have to go into the jungle.

He thought about taking Tin Oo along. But he

did not like to lose the time. Already it was late; Tin Oo would be having supper soon. And Tin Oo's mother and father would be worried and angry if Tin Oo went into the jungle—especially if U Gyi learned that his rule had been broken. But Grandfather will not miss me, he thought; I am late most of the time anyway. And U Gyi did not make his rule to keep me safe. He crowded out the lonely feeling which had come stealing in, saying to himself with a toss of his head, "I know something U Gyi does not: the tiger is far away on the other side of the jungle. Anyway, I want to go alone."

The jungle loomed before him. Shifting the ax to get a balanced hold, he set off. He moved swiftly among the giant bamboo, their stalks as big as a man, and parted the tough elephant grass; here and there encountering a banyan tree, he slipped under its many arms: they were like tentacles reaching out and down to clutch the earth. All these were familiar to him. He would have to go deep to find a stand of teakwood trees.

The forest darkened as he advanced, and the

jungle noises grew louder. Yellow birds in the hundreds were twittering in one tall banyan. He plowed along through the crackling leaves covering the ground. Something bright blue gleamed in a shaft of sunlight, and stooping, he saw it was a peacock's feather. He tucked it in his waist—it could decorate a costume.

His mind turned to thoughts of his puppets. Tomorrow he would take them to school so that the girls could dress them. He might even give the feather to Chit Chit for a minister's costume.

As he entered a clearing he heard a sharp sound; looking up, he saw a shining green parrot skim across the clearing. The spread of its wings, the angle of its head—it looked like his puppet parrot brought to life! All of a sudden a black, furry body sailed out of a tree, dropped to the ground and, curled in a little ball, rolled right to his feet. Ko Shway jumped back, startled. The ball unwound, and he saw first the skinny tail and then the little round head of a monkey. The monkey made a show of being startled, too, and chattering noisily, tumbled away. There is another

75

puppet, Ko Shway thought, laughing. He had an eerie feeling, as if he had stumbled onto a puppet stage, now big as life—as if he himself were a puppet.

As he plunged again into thick forest on the other side of the clearing, the fat branch of a tree began to move. A sleepy gray python was shifting its position. He is not in the puppet show, Ko Shway thought, shuddering, and moved quickly on.

Now the undergrowth was thinning, and the leafy carpet under his feet changed to hard-packed clay. Ahead of him was another clearing and beside it a stand of teak trees.

Delighted, he sprang forward and found that the clay under his feet had turned soft and gluey. In the center of the clearing was a muddy pool. And now he noticed scores of small hoofprints in the clay. The barking deer came here, he realized; it was a watering hole.

He hoped he would not have to cut a live tree. A fallen tree would be better seasoned. And he was in luck. Right at the edge of the clearing one tree had become uprooted and was leaning on another—not rotted—just right. He set to work chopping a piece large enough for the king's head, but not so large and heavy that he couldn't carry it.

He had not known how very hard teakwood could be. Yet, as he chopped he was happy, because he could tell by the feel of the wood that it would be perfect for carving. Swinging all his strength behind the ax, feeling the harsh jolt in his shoulders again and again, he was certain that he would be able to carve a head grand enough for a king.

The last fibers finally came away, and Ko Shway picked up the chunk of wood, running his hands, moist with effort, over the roughhewn surfaces. His face was salty wet, his bangs stuck to his forehead, and his shirt to his back. He was thirsty, and giving the piece of wood a loving pat, he at last looked up from his labors. There, at the water hole, a family of barking deer were drinking.

Ko Shway threw back his head and laughed aloud. The doe glanced in his direction, and then, not hurrying, but not wasting time either, the little family moved away.

"My turn," Ko Shway called after them, and ran to the water hole. As he knelt to drink, cupping the water in his hands, feeling the wet clay cool on his knees, his eye fell on something which made him freeze absolutely still. He stared at the ground and looked away and stared again, to be sure he was not mistaken in what he saw: it was the paw mark of a tiger.

But how could that be? The tiger had been way off in the jungle on the other side of the village that time when he had heard it call. It must have circled around, looking for water, perhaps—closing in on the village, perhaps! Let's see, how far am I from the village? An hour, maybe; maybe two?

He became aware of many eyes looking at him from beyond the clearing. It is the time for the animals to come to the water hole. And—will the tiger come? He scrambled up and grabbed his ax and his piece of teakwood. Looking warily around, expecting to see a flash of orange at any moment, he left the clearing and headed for home.

When he reached the edge of the jungle and the comfortable sight of his own banyan tree, the sun had set, the moon risen. All the way, stumbling and falling in his haste, he had been thinking. He knew he should warn someone that the tiger was very near. He should warn his grandfather or U Gyi. But if he did that, they would know that he had been in the jungle and that he had broken the rule. Now his earlier thinking did not seem to fit. Now he knew that U Gyi would be angry and his grandfather more discouraged than ever about him. He remembered what his grandfather had said about tigers and about Ko Shway's ignorance. I am only a boy, he realized now. Why did I think I had a right to break the rule?

Leaving the teakwood and the ax in his tree house, he ran all the way, across the rice paddies and through the village, to his home. His grandfather stood in the doorway peering into the dusk. As Ko Shway approached, his grandfather smiled, and putting his arm around the boy's shoulder, guided him into the house. "Where have you been, Ko Shway? It is so late. Never mind, never mind, I have saved some rice and curry for you. Sit, boy, and eat."

Hungry and tired and close to tears, Ko Shway ate.

It was all too easy to say nothing.

Chapter 6

The day of the puppet show arrived at last. In the school, the stage and the painted jungle backdrop were in place. All the puppets were painted and costumed. Ko Shway himself had put the robes and crown on King Anawrahta, whom he was keeping in his tree house. He wanted no one to see the king until the play began. If, deep inside himself, he worried about the tiger, he did not think about it.

Very early in the morning Ko Shway sped along past the rice fields to his tree house. He smiled at the water buffaloes grazing at the edge of the jungle under an arching limb of his banyan tree. As he began to climb, some monkeys set up a great clatter. Ko Shway stopped for a moment to imitate their sound and then climbed cheerily on.

Suddenly the jungle was quiet. "That's funny," Ko Shway said to himself, knowing that the jungle is never really quiet.

As he swung up into his tree house, a flock of jungle pheasants flew screaming past, and Ko Shway turned to see what had frightened them.

Then he saw the tiger!

It was about one hundred yards to the left of the banyan tree, creeping slowly, cautiously through the deep, dry grass at the edge of the jungle.

Ko Shway crouched absolutely still, not daring to move. His heart was beating wildly, and the jungle came alive with warning sounds heralding the approach of the tiger.

At first it seemed to Ko Shway that the tiger was coming straight to his banyan tree. But as he watched he realized that the tiger was stealing toward the water buffaloes! For a moment he watched, fascinated. How beautiful it was, its sleek coat quivering, its brilliant curving splashes of black and rust and white flashing in the deep grass. He could see its slim back flattened, the great joints of its shoulders hunched up, its huge head muzzling close to the ground.

The water buffaloes had not yet caught the scent. And when they do, Ko Shway thought, it will be too late.

Warning! Warning! I must give a warning! But how? He looked desperately around and saw his horn. Yes—but I must get closer. Clutching the horn, he began cautiously to climb up toward the limb which hung over the grazing water buffaloes.

Ko Shway crept; and the tiger crept. Ko Shway, hardly breathing, inched his way up the tree.

Grasping with his knees the end of the topmost

branch, he leaned way out and down, hanging as close as he could reach above the backs of the helpless water buffaloes. He held the horn to his lips and blew with all his breath.

The water buffaloes threw up their heads and started to run, lumbering and stumbling across the field toward the village. The tiger whirled, swung off to the side, tail lashing, and bounded into a bamboo thicket.

Very much relieved, Ko Shway thought about coming down. He must carry the news to the village. If he didn't tell this time everybody would be in danger. He thought fondly, protectingly of Daw Ma Ma, Tin Oo, Grandfather—Mi Mi, Chit Chit—even U Gyi and the others. This time he would not fail. But he was not sure where the tiger was. He could see the stalks of the bamboo moving ever so slightly. It might be there, and it might not. He was not sure. It did not seem a good plan, at this point, to come down. But if he did not, how would the village be warned?

The water buffaloes! They will warn the village. Then people will come. But what if they do come, not knowing about the tiger?

And what if they don't come? Should he climb
down and risk it? He couldn't decide.

In the village, the bazaar women were setting
out fruit and longyis in the stalls. Daw Ma Ma, on
her way to school, nodded and smiled a greeting as
she hurried past. Rounding a corner, she nearly
bumped into U Gyi, who was taking his morning
walk.

"Nice day," he said, bowing. "A little hot, perhaps," he added amiably.

"Yes, very," Daw Ma Ma agreed, anxious to be
going on.

Just then the commotion began—chickens

squawking, pigs running every which way, people angrily calling out. And then the water buffaloes lumbered into view.

"Oh, no! Not again!" U Gyi cried. He and Daw Ma Ma backed quickly under a tree as the water buffaloes, heaving and puffing, galloped past. U Gyi's face turned red and angry, and he said, "Daw Ma Ma, this is too much! That Ko Shway has stampeded my buffaloes again!"

"Oh, surely not, U Gyi," Daw Ma Ma protested. "I am quite sure Ko Shway would not do such a thing—not today. Today is the puppet show, you see," she explained.

But U Gyi was no longer listening. He had turned to watch the water buffaloes crashing through the bazaar.

Men, women, and children had begun to gather around. Taking charge, U Gyi said, "Some of you people, there—return these animals to the fields. I shall come along. I mean to find that boy, and when I do—" He didn't finish and his voice had risen almost to a shout. "Just wait till I get my hands on him!"

Daw Ma Ma gathered the children about her and instructed them to go to the schoolhouse to finish their preparations for the puppet show. She said she would come as soon as she could. Then she said firmly to U Gyi, "I am coming, too."

So they started off, U Gyi and Daw Ma Ma in the lead and almost the entire village following, prodding the confused water buffaloes with long sticks.

As the noisy procession drew near the field, the most unlikely sounds came from the direction of the jungle. "Shh." U Gyi held up his hands for silence. Everyone listened. The clacking and the blare of a horn could now be heard distinctly.

They looked toward the banyan tree where the noise seemed to be coming from. And there was Ko Shway! He was beating with a stick on the side of his tree house and blowing his horn.

"Stay back, everybody, stay back! There is a tiger in the bamboo!"

But U Gyi did not believe him. Thinking it one more of Ko Shway's jokes, he began to splutter, and started forward. Daw Ma Ma grabbed him by the arm, saying, "Wait." She had been thinking,

and the more she thought about Ko Shway and the puppet show and the tiger mask episode, the more it seemed to her that something special must be going on.

But U Gyi flung off her hand. He grabbed a long pole from a startled villager and strode angrily into the field.

"No, no, U Gyi," Ko Shway called out frantically. "Go back, please go back. There is a tiger. There really is." But U Gyi kept coming.

Ko Shway felt very sure now that the tiger was still in the bamboo, and he began to throw things from his tree house into the thicket. As the heavy objects rained down, the tiger finally moved. It appeared for a moment at the edge of the field and then disappeared into the jungle.

When he saw the tiger with his own eyes, U Gyi rushed back to where the villagers, quite frightened now, were clustered together. "All right, everyone," he said. "Go to your homes. Get pots, kettles, anything that will make a noise, and come back here. I will get my rifle. We must drive this tiger deep into the jungle."

Daw Ma Ma was looking around for Ko Shway, who was no longer in the tree. For a moment she was frightened. Then suddenly he emerged from the bamboo thicket, carrying a puppet. He ran to Daw Ma Ma. "Look," he said, grinning, "I had to send King Anawrahta to fight the tiger. He's wounded—his arm has come off. But he's all right. See?"

As the village men ran to their homes, Ko Shway and Daw Ma Ma walked slowly to the school. Together they decided that, in spite of all the excitement, it would be best to go ahead with the puppet show.

So, while the men of the village, led by U Gyi, went out to frighten away the tiger, the children of the village put on the best and only puppet show ever seen in Pinlebu. King Anawrahta was inspired, and with his arm in a sling, he conquered his enemies, though they threatened to come after him with ten thousand elephants.

After the puppet show, Mi Mi and Chit Chit helped Daw Ma Ma pass around rice cakes to the women and children. And Ko Shway had a chance

93

to tell Tin Oo all that had happened. Tin Oo listened with his mouth hanging open.

"Weren't you scared, Ko Shway?"

"Well, sure," Ko Shway answered, "especially when I was waiting for people to come. I thought maybe they wouldn't believe the tiger was real—this time."

Ko Shway took a deep, satisfied breath and bit into his rice cake. He looked around the schoolroom. Something, he was aware, had changed. The air was growing heavy and dark.

Absorbed as they all had been, no one had noticed that outside, dark clouds were forming, moving ponderously over the face of the sun. A breeze had sprung up and was banging the bamboo blinds.

Then Ko Shway heard a wonderful sound. "Listen," he cried. "It's beginning!" And then they all heard it—the first fat splashes of water, making splats on the thatched roof. The monsoon was beginning!

The children streamed out into the field. They danced about, shouting and catching water in

their cupped hands. Even Daw Ma Ma kicked off
her sandals and ran into the rain, laughing with
the other women. Faster and thicker it came, till
the air seemed turned to water.

Ko Shway's shirt stuck to his back, and he tied his longyi up high so that he could splash free in the pools of water forming all over the field.

And here came the men back from the jungle. They were singing, marching, and beating their pots in time. The tiger would never come back now—now that the monsoon had started.

The children ran to meet the men. U Gyi, catching sight of Ko Shway, called out, "Young man, today is a day to be proud of!"

"Hooray for Ko Shway," one of the men shouted.

They swung him on their shoulders and paraded into the village, laughing and singing and swishing through the wet. His grandfather came out of his house, smiling broadly and waving. And the rain splashed down on the upturned face of the boy who liked to be doing things, the boy who played tiger.